The Hare
And Other Stories

Catherine Fisher

Pont Books

First Publication—April 1994
Second Impression—October 1995
Third Impression—1997

ISBN 1 85902 176 X

© Catherine Fisher

Published with the support of the Welsh Arts Council.

Printed by J.D. Lewis & Sons, Ltd.,
Gomer Press, Llandysul, Dyfed

Contents

The Hare

'I'm sure they can arrest us for this.' Owen shoved his hands into his pockets and kicked at the muddy bank. 'Any archaeologist would go mad. This is some sort of barrow.'

'Was. Caer Ceridwen it was called, but it was ploughed out years ago. The stuff's all in Cardiff museum.' His uncle's hands were rough with the slim machine; he swept it like a scythe, a long, low cut through the air. It bleeped, suddenly.

'There!' Jack Hughes stubbed his boot into the furrow. 'Try there.'

Reluctantly Owen crouched again, out of the wind that whistled up through the trees and the black spines of the hedgerow. The soil was frozen on top, but under that it was still soft, like fudge. He sliced the trowel through it. The top of a beer can glinted.

His uncle swore, briefly. 'Well, that's it. It's not over here.'

He turned his back on the wind, pulled a handful of grubby items out of his pocket and picked mud off them. 'Let's see what we've got. An old shilling; a nail; a lump of lead.'

'Could be a plumbob,' Owen suggested.

His uncle weighed it in his hand. 'Could be. Or a fishing weight, but then how did it get up here? Must be a story to that. Two tin can tops; a bolt—from a tractor, I should think. And then this.'

The last was a thin disc about the size of a saucer,

covered with a blue-white powder that came off on his hands. He examined it. 'Could be anything. Looks old.'

Owen frowned. 'If it's out of that barrow . . .'

'Look, I told you, they dug that up in the forties. I should know, I spent most of my school time watching. It was big then, but look at it now.'

Owen nodded. The corner of the field was a muddy mass of hillocks and ruined ditches. The humped earth in the centre was still shoulder-high, but scarred and pocked with cavities, sprouting dock and brambles.

Jack Hughes shouldered the metal detector. 'Now as for that ring of your mother's—you'll have to get her to come up here and show me the exact spot. This is a twelve-acre field and we can't go over it all. I've got to give this machine back, you know.'

'I know.' Owen threw the rubbish into one of the ditches. Then, after second thoughts, he picked it out again and pushed it into his coat pocket.

They walked around the humps and hollows of the ruined barrow and climbed the gate. His uncle turned towards the farm. 'Tell her, mind. Sunday would be best. I'll have a bit more time then.'

'Right.'

'And if we're arrested you can come and break us out of jail.'

Owen grinned, and turned away down the lane.

The wind met him at the corner, leaping into his face like an exhuberant dog. Down below, the valley curved into its great wooded horseshoe, the swift river glinting through it, the houses strung out along the road to Llandogo. There too, in its green field on the riverbank, stood the roofless abbey, its arches rising like stone fingers placed delicately together at the tips. It always seemed unfinished, he thought, not ruined; it was so neat, with its mown grass, and the pillars and buttresses springing into the vast windy spaces of the nave, open to the sky and its scudding clouds. Through the east window he could see the dark woods on the crag, and a faint crescent moon hanging over them.

The lamps were lit in Tintern; the last tourist coach roaring out of the car park. He took the muddy little footpath along the river and then ran through the huddle of houses to one with a green door and a stunted rosemary bush outside it.

'At last!' his mother shouted from the kitchen, as he slammed the door. 'Your tea's nearly frazzled. Hurry up.'

He sat at the table, pushing his sister's school books aside.

'Where are they?'

'Chepstow. They went in for the shopping.' She came in and dropped a hot plate in front of him. 'Did Jack find my ring?'

'No.' He explained quickly, between mouthfuls.

'Ah well,' his mother sighed, flitting past the door with a frying pan in her hand. 'It's all a lost hope if you ask me. I'd love to find it, but it's like looking for a needle in a haystack.'

Owen knew she was still upset. 'It'll turn up,' he said firmly. 'We'll find it.'

When he had finished he took his coat upstairs and tipped out the finds on the bed. None of them were any use. Then he picked up the disc and looked at it carefully. It was certainly metal of some sort, beaten thin, corroding and crumbling away at the edges. Not iron. Might it be silver? He rubbed the surface gently with his sleeve. There were marks on it, very thin incised lines; he could make out a circle, and a crescent, then some lines that whirled around each other, spirals and waves. And at the edge scratches, like strange stick-like letters. Nothing that made sense.

Downstairs, the door slammed. He wrapped the disc in his school scarf and put it into the top drawer. Then he threw the rest of the stuff in the bin.

'Owen!' his sister screeched up the stairs. 'Come and see this! Quick!'

She sounded so excited that he went down deliberately slowly, one step at a time.

They were all in the kitchen; his father was holding

something heavy, wrapped up in the plaid rug from the car. Owen hurried over.

'What is it?'

'A hare. The car must have hit it. Clear all those books off the table, Becky.'

Carefully, he laid the bundle down, put a hand inside and gripped tight. Then he pulled away the rug.

The hare crouched on the table, body rigid, ears flat. It was white, in full winter coat, its huge round eyes black in the dim room, with the firelight flickering deep in them like tiny red stars. It was a large creature, its strong back legs braced against the table.

'White!' Owen said. 'That's odd.'

'It certainly is.' His father eased his grip gently. 'It might be an albino; you don't get mountain hares round here.'

The hare stared out at nothing. Its ears twitched.

'Doesn't seem to be hurt.' Mr Lewis felt over its skin carefully. 'Nothing broken. Just shock, I suppose. The way it loomed up in the road was terrifying—a white flicker in the moonlight, just on that bend by the quarry where the trees are thickest. I didn't feel a thump, but when we stopped the car and went back it was just sitting there, looking at us.'

'I think we went right over it,' Rebecca said. She reached out and touched the animal. It did not move

12

as she slowly smoothed the stiff fur of its neck, and she smiled at the feel of it. 'Will it be all right?'

'Oh yes. We'll leave it in here tonight, in the warm. The cat can sleep in the shed for once. Now don't make a fuss of it, Beck.'

'I won't,' she said. But still her fingers stroked it, over and over.

All evening the hare lay in the box of straw by the fire. Rebecca gave it some water and a few lettuce leaves but it did not even sniff them. She and Owen played chess, and between moves she smoothed the hare and spoke to it, but it never turned its head. It sat still in the straw, watching the flickering firelight.

'Checkmate,' Owen said at last.

Rebecca turned. 'Well . . . no, it's not. I can go there.'

He tapped the bishop. 'Still in check. Your own fault. You can't concentrate because of that animal.' He got up, yawning. 'Listen to the wind.'

The gale had been rising all evening; now it howled and hummed against the windows. A door upstairs was banging in the draught.

'There's nothing forecast.' Their father folded the newspaper, and threw it down. 'Hopeless, these weathermen. Now, time you went up into the hills.'

That was always his way of telling them to go to bed. Owen said goodnight and opened the door into the hall. A sudden gale of wind rattled against the windows.

'Coming from the west,' his father remarked. Owen nodded. As he went out he noticed the hare turn its head, for the first time. It looked at him. Its eyes were black.

It was very late when Owen woke. The small gilt clock down in the hall was pinging quietly and he counted the strokes. Only three. But it had been some other noise that had woken him, not the clock, or even the wind that was roaring over the roof. Something else.

He lay still. The room was dim, the window a paler square of darkness. He could see a star through a gap in the curtains, and the glow of next-door's porch light. Far off, a car droned up the valley. Then he sat up, leaning one elbow on the pillow. There it was again—a low creak, coming from somewhere in the house.

The flesh on the back of his neck prickled.

He swung his feet out into the cold air, pulled on trainers and dressing-gown and quietly opened the door. The landing was silent, its furniture dark masses of shadow. His sister's door was open, just a slit, and he paused by it and breathed 'Beck?' No answer.

At the top of the stairs he waited, his hand tight on

the smooth white ball of the bannister, his heart thumping softly.

The house stirred around him, its familiar creaks and sighs and ticks unheard. Nor the wind under the doors. It was the other sound he was waiting for, that long, oddly familiar creak of movement.

Inch by inch, silent, he came down the stairs. The kitchen door was open; a strange pale light flooded out onto the telephone table and the vase of evergreens, silvering his face as he crept nearer, and his hand as it reached out for the knob.

In the room, something was moving.

Without breathing, he edged the door wider and put his eye to the crack.

The kitchen was bright with moonlight; the curtains had been tugged back and an enormous full moon made the room a web of black and silver. Long rectangles of moonlight lay on the table and the newspapers and his chess pieces frozen in their game. He could see only half of the room; the fireplace with its cinders, the window, the dresser. Then the sweat on his back turned to ice.

A white hand had come out of the darkness and taken hold of the drawer handle; a long thin hand with delicate fingers. Slowly it drew the drawer open and began to dip and rustle inside, picking up forks and curtain rings and a watch, and dropping them back with a click. As it pulled out a small mirror of his mother's, there was a pause; he heard a sound like an indrawn breath. Then the mirror was flung back. He could only see the hands, and the edge of a pale sleeve, trimmed with fur.

The wind flung itself against the house; a window banged. In a surge of panic Owen slammed the door wide and snapped on the light. In the sudden dazzle something twisted and blurred and scuttled on the floor. He stared down at it.

The hare was sitting upright, looking at the moon. It seemed bigger; the fur around its neck was bristling and stiff. It turned its head and gazed at him, and sudden fear churned inside him like the wind whirling round the house. For a second the stare held him, then he jerked back, slammed the door tight, turned the key and hurtled up the stairs.

His mother's voice caught him on the landing. 'Owen? What's wrong?'

'Nothing.' He was shaking; he gripped the brass rail of his bed and it was ice in his hot palms. 'Nothing. I just went down for a drink.'

In the morning, Mr Lewis carried the box outside and set it down under the hedge. The grass was rigid with frost, and crunched underfoot. Owen, still chewing his toast, waited on the path.

'I still think it's a bit soon,' Rebecca complained. 'I thought we could keep it for a bit.'

Her father shrugged. 'Owen's right. It's not a pet.'

She turned and made a face at Owen but he ignored her. He was watching his father lift the creature out onto the frosty grass. The hare flattened its ears. It flopped one pace forward, and sat down.

'Off you go,' Mr Lewis muttered.

But the hare sat still.

'It doesn't want to go,' Becky murmured.

Go, Owen thought fiercely. Whatever you are, go, run away. Leave us alone.

Mr Lewis stepped back. 'Leave it now. It'll soon go when it wants to.'

Owen went in and sat at the window, pretending to read. He was tired; he had spent the rest of the night sitting up in bed, listening to every creak in the house, every gust of wind, imagining the hare flopping up the stairs in the dark, waking with a crick in his neck at half past six, when the horses from the riding school clopped past outside. And he hadn't told anyone. He couldn't.

All morning he watched the hare. It didn't go; he knew it wouldn't. It sat still in the melting frost, nose to the sky, the wind ruffling its fur. Not an animal, something else, something other. Something wicked. He began to hate the sight of it, but he could not read, or get up or go out. It held his eyes with a real undefined fear. He hadn't dreamed that cold hand searching in the drawer. He had looked in

17

there this morning—it was a mess, but that was normal. Still, he had seen it. It had been looking for something. He remembered the web of moonlight, silver and black.

At last Rebecca marched down the stairs. 'Well I'm not leaving that animal out there,' she announced. 'It must be stunned.'

She unlatched the door.

'Don't!' Owen leapt up, nearly tipping the chair over. 'Leave it alone!'

She stared at him in astonishment. 'Don't be daft. What's all the fuss?'

'Don't let it back into the house, Beck.'

'Why not?'

She was watching him with a strange hostile look. How could he tell her? She would only laugh at him. He shrugged. 'It gives me the creeps. It's not normal.'

She stared. 'You're mad, Owen.'

She went out and carried the hare in. 'The poor thing's dazed, that's all; it needs more time to recover. One more night should do it.'

One more night, Owen thought grimly. He watched her fingers smoothing the white fur; her face reflected in the hare's huge, upturned eyes.

Later, in the cloisters of the abbey, the sun was warm on the stones. Owen leaned his head back and

18

watched the tourists taking photographs in the nave, scattered in groups on the carpet of green grass. Year in, year out, the abbey stood there and the people came. Didn't they have ruined churches anywhere else, he wondered. Or poets that wrote about them?

He glanced up at the crag of the Devil's Pulpit on the English side of the river. It was the stories that brought them, of course. The tales of monks and witches and real people who had lived long ago, and the trees, armies of them, guarding the border. Up there the devil had screamed at the monks, thrown rocks, they said. All nonsense, of course. The trees up there were bending now, in the gale. A thin moon, faint as a smudge of chalk, hung over them.

The sight of it sat him bolt upright with shock.

The moon!

LAST NIGHT IT HAD BEEN FULL!

He remembered it clearly, the huge circle of silver, the dark smudges of its seas and mountains.

What did it mean? How could the moon change or a hare be anything but a hare?

He shook his head and scrambled up, walking quickly through the arches into the booking office packed with shelves of mugs and tea towels and CADW guidebooks, out through the swing door, then breaking into a run along the river, as it swirled brown and swift under the hanging woods. Past the houses, across the road, dodging the cars, then up the lane to the farm, running hard now, dragging in breath as he raced uphill. The wind was with him, it pushed and buffetted him on, up the steep muddy lane between its hawthorns and hollies.

The drone of the tractor met him at Cae Mawr; he leapt on the gate and waved, then swung over and raced across the furrows.

His uncle leaned out of the cab. 'You'll get covered in mud.'

'Never mind,' he gasped. 'Listen . . . that barrow.'

His uncle grinned. 'Still thinking about that?'

'But listen! Whose was it? What did they find in it?'

Jack Hughes climbed down and lit a cigarette. Smoke streamed out in the wind. 'Well not that much. They were female remains, I remember that. Old, maybe Bronze Age. There were a lot of little bits and pieces; ornaments, a buckle, brooches and the like. Most of it was badly corroded—just looked like little blue scraps to me, when they showed me. The best thing was a big cauldron, and there was a broken axle from a cart.'

'But you said it was called . . .'

'. . . Caer Ceridwen. Yes. Ceridwen's Fort. Oh you remember her, in one of those old folktales. She was a witch, a shapeshifter, maybe even a goddess. She turned herself into different creatures, hunting that lad who stole the magic from her cauldron.' He

20

gazed out into the wind. 'Strange now, that this place should have had a woman's name all this time, and then to find a real woman in it. Where are you off to now?'

But Owen was already climbing the gate. 'Home,' he shouted. Then he turned. 'In that story. Did she catch him?'

'She caught him.' Jack Hughes yelled over the field. 'There's no escaping her.'

The lanes were already darkening; the wind rising again and howling down the valley in all the moving branches of the trees. The lights of a cottage down a track flickered on as Owen raced by; glancing back he saw something pale glimmer in the lane behind him. For a second he saw it clearly; a white hare sitting upright in the shelter of the hedge. Then the wind gusted, flapping his coat collar and blowing dust into his eyes so that they watered and suddenly the road ran with flickering shapes; a slim dog, an otter, a flapping hawk, blurring one into the other, nearer and nearer under the roaring trees. Owen turned and fled into the darkness, racing along the lane, down the hill, round the corner, breathless and aching to the giddy lip of the valley where he clung, winded, to a gatepost.

Below, the abbey was a black net pierced with arches; beside it the river glinted with moonlight.

Clouds moved on its rippling surface. Like a mirror, he thought, clutching his side. Like a mirror.

The village was dark as he stumbled down between the houses; the light from the kitchen dazzled him as he flung the door open and almost fell inside.

The box by the fire was empty!

'Where's the hare?' he gasped.

His father glanced over the newspaper. 'It's there, isn't it?'

Fear clutching him, Owen ran into the hall.

The hare was waiting at the top of the stairs; its white fur glistening, its eyes dark holes. It flopped slowly past him down the steps.

He ran up into his mother's bedroom. Every drawer and cupboard was open; clothes and jewellery were strewn on the bed and the floor.

Hurriedly, he picked things up, shoved them back. The others mustn't know. Whatever happened, they mustn't. He knew now it was his fault, that he would have to sort it out.

When it was done he went down and ate his tea. The hare was in its box, eyes staring into the flames. He sat opposite it, grimly.

Outside, the gale howled and lashed at the walls. The windows thrummed like taut wire.

His father came in at nine. 'The Anchor's closed early,' he said. 'River's rising fast—it must be raining higher up. And the wind in the abbey sounds like a choir of voices. I'd better put the shutters up on the back windows.'

All evening Owen watched the hare and the hare watched him.

His mother laughed at the television; Rebecca lay curled in a chair with a book. Every now and then she reached down and stroked the white fur; once it moved, uneasily, and the wind screamed in the chimney.

All night Owen was never alone with it. Even when he tried to be the last up he was so tired that his mother made him go to bed. He splashed some water on his face, went into the bedroom, sat on his bed and waited.

The shapes of animals, flowing one into another, moved under his eyelids.

At half past two a sound jerked him awake. Furious with himself he opened the door quickly and peered out.

The house was humming in the wind; the door to his sister's room was wide and moonlight was pouring through it. Clutching something in his hand he went in.

Rebecca lay asleep, the pale light streaming over her. Next to the bed, looking down, stood a woman, tall, her hair woven into elaborate braids. She wore a straight white dress pinned with a silver brooch at each shoulder. Her hand was stretched out; she had picked up a lock of Becky's brown hair from the pillow and was fingering it.

She looked up; her eyes dark and venomous. Behind her he glimpsed the open wardrobe; the crumpled clothes flung on the floor.

'Leave her alone,' he muttered.

The woman's eyes were black in the moonlight. 'Give me my mirror,' she said.

'Leave her alone. Leave us all alone and I'll give it to you.'

He brought his hand out from behind his back and held it out to her; the thin silver disc with its moon-marks and lost unreadable words. She moved quickly, but he drew back.

'Promise first. You'll never come again.'

'It was you who came.' She came towards him; her face was narrow, her lips pale in the unearthly light. 'You came and took what was mine. I am the pursuer. I have hunted you down and found you.'

She was so close he could feel the coldness of her, the icy draughts from her skin.

'Promise,' he muttered, his fingers clenched tight on the disc.

She was silent a moment. Then she nodded. 'Very well,' she said.

She took the mirror out of his hand, and it glittered as she lifted it and looked in, and Owen saw her face, to his astonishment, perfectly mirrored, as if the corroded metal was polished smooth. She turned it, and he saw himself, small and white-faced, and behind him the moon, huge in the window, and out there was the valley, dark and shaggy with trees, the abbey gone, the houses gone; only the trees, crowding to the river's edge, their dark undergrowth riddled with the paths of wolf and boar.

'We are all in here,' she said. 'Beast, man, spirit. Water and tree. Those who come and those who go. All reflected, as if in a tale or a story.'

The metal slowly clouded.

Then there was only the hare, sitting white and still on the bedroom carpet.

After a moment Owen turned and went downstairs, then through the kitchen to the back door. As he opened it the cold wind struck him.

The hare flopped past him and sat on the doorstep, its great eyes staring out into the banging, flapping darkness.

'I'm sorry,' Owen said abruptly. 'About the barrow. I'll try and get them not to go there again.'

The hare looked at him. Then it bolted into the dark.

Before he closed the door Owen put his head out and looked down at the abbey. A thin half-moon balanced on its black shoulder. As he turned he felt something cold as ice under his foot; it lay on the doorstep gleaming, and he bent and picked it up.

It was his mother's ring.

Ghost in the Rain

Every year, since I was eight, I've come to stay at Maes-y-rhiw for the summer. It is a long journey, especially as I have to travel on my own, but the first glimpse of the old red-brick house on its knoll, with the lake reflecting it like a mirror, always gives me a warm, safe, happy feeling.

I remember the first time I came. That time it was by train. I stood outside the station, pressed into the hedge as the carts and cattle crowded by to the market at Trenewydd. My bag was very heavy; I put it down in the dust and looked hopefully up the lane at the small dogcart rattling towards me, its pony trotting between the high hedges. When it pulled up, a tall dark-haired woman in a grey habit was looking down at me.

'I suppose you must be Sarah?'

I nodded, nervously. 'That's right.'

'I'm your Aunt Alicia. I won't eat you. Is that your bag?' She had it on the seat next to her already; she moved very quickly and abruptly, just as she spoke. 'In you get.' Climbing up, I saw her glance over me critically; my frock, stockings, shoes and new blue coat. Then she flicked the pony into a walk. 'You're very neat. How old are you?'

'Eight, aunt.'

'Can you dress yourself, and all that?'

I looked at her in surprise, and she caught my eye. 'Well, good,' she said with a laugh. 'I've no nanny or nurse at Maes-y-rhiw. Mrs Powell is the cook but she's got no time to fuss and fidget over a great girl like you. And I have my work. I'm afraid you'll have to amuse yourself for much of the time. Try not to get into scrapes, won't you?'

My mother had warned me about this. Aunt Alicia was an artist; she painted landscapes and portraits and even had them shown in big exhibitions in London and Cardiff. I like to paint and draw too. My tutor, Mr Waterhouse, had even said to my mother that I had talent, and safe in my bag, packed flat among my nightdresses, were two of my best sketches that I had brought for my aunt to see. I remember how I rubbed the seams of my new white gloves, and wondered if I would dare show them.

Then we turned a corner of the lane, and there was the house, with red creeper smothering the brick-work, and the house-martins skimming and shriek-ing in the hot blue sky.

Well, I was right. I never did get to show her those drawings. I soon found that my mother had warned me well; Aunt Alicia had no time for me, no time for anything except her work. I only saw her at meal-times, and sometimes not even then, for if it was fine Mrs Powell would let me take bread and cheese and an apple into the garden and eat there, swinging in the pliant cedar branches. It was Mrs Powell who looked after me, as far as anyone did, but most of the time I was free to wander where I wanted; I could have left the grounds and walked for miles over the fields, and no one would even have noticed.

But it was the garden that I loved, and I still do. Every time I come here I spend most of my time out there. This year, as always, I've come back in the height of summer, when the afternoons are long and hot, and the butterflies dance in the heated borders, in a haze of phlox and delphinium.

The part of the garden I like best is the small walled garden to the south of the house. A high brick wall shelters it; trees and shrubs make it shady and secret. I've always had it to myself—Aunt Alicia never goes in. But this year, someone else was there.

I saw him first on the night I arrived.

The room I always have is on the corner of the house; a small room with pink wallpaper and heavy dark furniture. I was sitting on a cushion on the windowsill, looking down. It was about nine o'clock. The great cedar that grew by the wall was a black mass, rustling faintly. Beyond it the garden lay in shadow, a whisper of scents and stirrings. An owl flew over the wall and away to the wood beyond. The night was so still that I could hear the horses in the stable, shifting in their straw.

It was then I saw him.

He looked about thirteen. He stepped out from the bushes onto the grass, almost below my window, so that the light from the drawing room lit the side of his face and his fair hair. For a moment I thought he was peeping in; then he turned and ran over the lawn, silently.

In the corner where the trees grew thick and dark, there was an old well. No one used it. A low stone coping had been built around it years ago, and the shaft was closed with a wooden lid, green now and half rotten. It was a dank, unlucky place.

I watched as the boy walked around the well, looking down. Once he turned a pale face to the house, and then paused, resting both hands on the stone brim. He wore a white shirt that glimmered against the branches.

I stood up, suddenly uneasy.

The boy had lifted the edge of the cover; he slid it back, slowly, as if it was heavy, and leaned over and looked down. I imagined the darkness down there, the horrible stagnant smell, the slimy walls. Perhaps he was trying to see his reflection, or had dropped something, because now he was leaning out, leaning too far, and a thread of fear squirmed in me. I gripped the window frame.

'Be careful!' I hissed. 'You'll fall!'

His head jerked up; I saw him stare at the house, his eyes moving along the row of windows. I turned, ran out into the corridor and down the long, curving stair to the hall. The garden door was ajar; I slipped through, round the side of the house and under the rose arch.

The garden was empty.

Very slowly, I walked across the lawn to the well.

The cover lay to one side. I looked down. There was nothing but darkness, and a smell, as I had thought, a bitter tang of decay. Knee-deep in the long grass I looked around. Behind me, only one line of footprints marked the dew on the lawn.

After breakfast next morning Aunt Alicia went out. From the morning room I watched her climb into her carriage. She looked older this year; her hair was quite grey now, and she moved slowly, like someone with a secret sorrow. I had noticed it come on her two years ago, this sudden aging.

When the carriage had gone I went out into the garden, and spent the morning swinging in the cedar tree. I was quite used to being by myself, but I wondered a great deal about the boy. Who was he, and what had interested him so much about the well?

Below me, waist-deep in the lavender and roses, Siôn, the old man who looked after the garden, leaned on his fork. He was talking to his grandson, the farm boy who brought the eggs. I saw them glance towards the well, and, suddenly curious, I slid down a little, feeling the pliant branches dip under my weight.

'. . . almost three years ago,' the old man was saying.

'I remember, Taid. I was here, that night.'

'And it's changed her. She blames herself. Thinks if she'd had more time for the child, see? But she was always busy. There, it happened Ben, it can't be undone.'

Ben nodded, scratching his ear. 'And what you said in the Lion, taid, about . . . you know . . .'

'Now don't go repeating what I said in the Lion, boy, or I'll lose this situation and never get another, not at my age. There's no call for gossip.' Siôn ran one finger inside his dirty collar. 'Still, it's true, for all that. There's times now, when I'm working here alone, maybe in the afternoon like, or after tea, when I know someone is watching me. Someone silent. And it's worse by that well.'

'It would be,' Ben said, eyes wide.

'And I'll tell you something else. If I've nailed that well-cover down once I've nailed it a score of times. But if you went over there now, you could lift it, easy as easy.' He shook his head. 'That night they brought that poor little mite's body up, I knew how it would be.'

He stopped then, and perhaps he'd heard me,

because soon after they moved away, round the side of the house.

I sat there, quite still. So old Siôn thought that the garden was haunted. And it was true, I knew it was true. After a moment I climbed down, getting green smears from the bark on my hands and dress, and dropped lightly into the grass.

The well was dark, as always. Trees hung over it, and ivy swarmed up the sides. No sunlight ever came here; the grass was still wet, and snails, colonies of them, were clustered on the stones. The old man had been right about the cover; I slid it aside, easily.

Looking down, there was my face, small and white in the black ring of water, and behind me the green branches, filling the sky.

Then I stood up, and turned quickly.

The boy was leaning against a tree, a few yards away. He wore the same clothes, and his face was pale and narrow. He was watching me intently.

'Hello,' I said.

'Hello.' He straightened and came forward, stopping just out of touching distance. 'Who are you?'

'Sarah. Aren't you a bit cold, with no coat?'

He shrugged. 'Not really.'

I wondered whether to say that I had seen him the night before, but decided not to. He came up to the well and put his hands among the ivy and looked over.

'I think someone once drowned here,' I said, slowly, dragging the hair from my cheek. The wind moved the branches above us; spots of rain pattered on the leaves.

'Drowned?' The boy looked at me, and moved closer. His hands were thin, the fingers dirty with broken nails. 'Imagine, falling down there.' Together, we looked down. 'Imagine it,' he muttered. 'You'd kick and struggle and scream and no one would come, and then you'd go under, in the black water, and under again . . .'

I shuddered. 'You didn't tell me your name.'

'Huw. Meredith. I'm staying here.'

I stared at him. 'Are you?'

'Yes.' He came closer, put out a hand. I forced myself to stand still, but as his fingers came closer to my sleeve he said, 'You shouldn't be afraid. Not of the well . . .'

'Child! Come away from there!'

We both turned. Mrs Powell was standing at the drawing-room window, her dress and shawl flapping. 'Come here!' she said angrily.

I looked at the boy.

'Tonight,' he said. 'I'll wait for you here. At ten.'

All afternoon it rained, beating the flowers flat and rolling from the leaves into the soaking grass. The lake was a darkness between the trees, its surface dimpled with rain, and from all the downstairs windows in turn I watched the drops slide and patter down the glass. Even after tea, when the sky darkened and the wind dropped, even then the rain fell, in light taps and trickles of sound outside the house.

I waited until I heard Mrs Powell serve my aunt's supper. Then I opened the door of my bedroom and slipped out. The corridor was gloomy, its ends invisible. The great staircase curved down into the dimness, and peering through its smooth, twisted bannisters I could see one candle burning down there, on the sideboard by the mirror.

I came down, silently.

The only sound was the clock, its deep 'tock' and the soft click and stir of the invisible pendulum.

Half-way along the hall a slot of red, flickering light fell across the darkness; the drawing-room door was open. Hidden in the heavy purple folds of curtain I looked in at Aunt Alicia, sitting on the sofa before the fire. She did not see me. Her hair was untidy; wisps of it hung down and she wound them absently around her fingers. The room was littered with unfinished paintings, and sketches piled on the tables. She looked as people do sometimes when they don't know they are being watched; tired and unguarded, her back straight and her gaze hard and empty.

I tip-toed across the doorway, quickly, and ran down the kitchen passage to the garden door. It was ajar again. Rain was pattering into a pool on the doorstep, but when I stepped outside and looked up the cloud was broken and ragged, with dark patches of sky glinting with stars. Between the bushes the ground was muddy; water drops fell in showers from the springy branches.

The boy was waiting by the well; he was sitting on the edge, his shirt a glimmer in the darkness. He stood up as I crossed the lawn, and smiled.

'I knew that you'd come.'

'I said I would.' Carefully, I sat on the wet stone. 'You've opened the well.'

'It's easy to open.' He stepped closer, looking down. 'I always come here.'

'Why?'

He gave me a strange, sidelong glance. 'Do you know what I think? I think there are countries down there somewhere; that if you climb down far enough you might come to places with castles and where the animals can talk, and where ogres are. Don't you think so? Like the stories where the youngest son always comes off best.'

'I don't know,' I said, doubtfully. 'Perhaps.'

'I wish there were.' He scowled down at his reflection. 'I used to be a youngest son.'

'Used to be?'

He stood up, quickly. 'I hate it here. It's all so old, and so dull and no one speaks to you and there's nothing to do. I've wanted to go home for ages, but I can't. Not yet. It will be different now though, now you've come.' He looked at me, eagerly. 'I'll have someone to play with, someone to talk to. Do you climb trees?'

'All the time.'

The wind moved the branches around us, spattering raindrops down the well. Our far-off reflections rippled and blurred.

'And there's no need to be afraid of ghosts,' he said suddenly. 'Is there.'

'I don't think so,' I said. 'I'll come tomorrow, if you like.'

'Promise?'

'Promise.'

And I smiled at him, and let myself disappear very slowly, so as not to alarm him.

The Silver Road

Tom opened his eyes. He lay still for another minute, staring up at the ceiling, listening to the increasingly restless sounds from the other bed. Finally he heaved the bedclothes aside and got up. Weariness surged over him as he crossed the room.

Simon was asleep, curled under the blue quilt, twitching and muttering. Tom looked at the tiny gleaming hands of the clock. Quarter to three. Bang on time.

He bent over and took a fold of warm pyjama sleeve between finger and thumb. 'Si. Simon. Wake up.'

The movement stopped, with one small shudder. Simon lay still, facing the wall.

'Are you awake?' Tom whispered.

'Yes.'

Tom went for his dressing-gown, hanging on the back of the door. He paused, listening, but there was no sound from his mother's bedroom. He dragged the dressing-gown on, glad of its warmth, then came and sat on Simon's bed, pulling the quilt over his cold feet.

'Do you want the light on?'

'Yes.'

When the lamp clicked on a soft yellow glow showed them the familiar room, its huddle of clothes on the window-seat, the pictures of ships, the cloud of mobiles that hung and drifted from the ceiling—Simon's flock of carved, multicoloured birds.

Simon lay silent for a moment, then turned over and sat up against the pillow, pushing the long fair hair out of his eyes. He looked very tired. Tom nudged the bedclothes. 'Keep warm. Did you manage to touch the road this time?'

Simon shrugged. 'The road is the same—it always is. Smooth and silver and cold underfoot. I remembered to touch it like you said, but I'm still not sure what it's made of.' He yawned and rubbed one eye. 'You'd better get the book.'

Tom bent down, opened the cupboard and pulled out an old history exercise book half full of empty pages. He turned them, noting the date of each entry, sometimes in his neat round writing, ragged with sleeplessness, sometimes in Simon's spiky scrawl. They had written in it every night for two months.

He took a pen out of the drawer and wrote Thursday 23rd May 2.45 and then looked up at his step-brother.

'I walked along the road,' Simon said quietly, 'towards the wood. I was just where I had been last night. The road went downhill. This time it was raining—big heavy spots. I soon got wet.'

Still writing Tom said, 'Were those birds there?'

41

'No. There was just cloud; grey and low. I walked quickly and even ran but it seemed to take ages to get anywhere—it always does. The moon came up, on my right. The wood got closer, very slowly. There was no sound but the rain.'

'What was on each side of the road?' Tom asked. A sound in the other bedroom made them stop and listen, but after a while Simon whispered. 'The same. Hillsides of grass. And bushes—blackthorn, rowan, hawthorn, some others. And a few trees.'

Tom jotted it down quickly.

'It seemed to take me about an hour.' Simon went on, winding a corner of the sheet around his finger. 'Then I got to the wood. It was very dark in there; the road ran straight in through the trees, I could see it shining down in the dimness. I thought I'd have to go on, but I could hear water trickling and I wanted to see where it was—I was very thirsty all of a sudden. Then I saw a stream—like the others a few nights ago. It was bubbling up and running through the grass not far from the road, over some stones. It was very clear . . .'

He stared thoughtfully at the drifting mobiles. In the dim light their shadows wandered the ceiling. Outside a lorry strained up the hill and rattled into the distance.

Tom looked up. 'Go on. What happened?'

'I wanted a drink. I walked right to the edge of the

42

road.' He sat up suddenly and stared at Tom. 'But I had that feeling. Exactly the same ... my heart pounding and my hands all sweaty. I knew if I stepped off that road Tom, I was lost. Just lost.'

Tom watched him for a moment. He was almost too tired to think. They both were. For a moment he even felt a bitter twinge of envy. Why did he never dream of this place?

Simon lay back. 'And that's it. I woke up. Maybe just in time.'

There was silence in the room. Tom finished writing and glanced back over the pages. 'We're still no nearer knowing what causes it, or what to do.'

'I just want it to stop.'

They both did. At first it had been a joke, something to laugh about, but now it was a worry, a secret, growing fear. Now they only spoke about it to each other, and Tom often caught himself puzzling about it, at meals, on the bus, in lessons. He found it hard to concentrate on anything any more. Simon was good at art, he played the violin, everyone said he was the imaginative one, but this wasn't right. It wasn't normal. He cleared the worried look from his face. 'It'll go.'

'It had better.' Simon said simply. 'How long can we go without sleeping properly? And I know there's something waiting for me Tom. Someone at the end of that road.' He closed his eyes and rolled over. 'It's not just a dream. It's real.'

Tom closed the book. His hands were cold. After a moment he put the lamp out.

* * *

'A dream?' Ieuan Lewis said, swinging one leg over the table. 'A continuous dream?'

'Night after night.' Tom tossed his half-eaten sandwich into the metal bin marked "Adran Gelf" and stared out of the window at the pupils of Ysgol Llanharan running out of the rain. 'And it's so real. He's really there, and he can remember it, not like ordinary dreams. Even the weather is real.'

The bell silenced him; its electric scream made them both jump slightly, although they'd been expecting it. When it stopped, Ieuan twisted a strand of his hair between a cobalt thumb and a yellow-splashed finger. 'I always thought Simon had talent,' he said, 'but . . . come and look at this.'

Ieuan was the art master. He was also Tom's first cousin, and not one of his teachers, which made things easy between them. He rummaged among a pile of folders and pulled one out with Simon Owein Jones scrawled across it in chalk, and out of it took a painting that Tom stared at in astonishment.

The silver road ran between boulders on a high hillside. Streams ran beside it glinting; on each side, in Simon's intricate brushwork, were gorse bushes,

44

bracken, high banks of hawthorn, bright blue hare-bells. Butterflies danced in the pale sky. The empty road ran down to a distant wood, and beyond it the horizon was a blue wash, with a suggestion of far misty hills, blurring into the white paper.

'I thought it was a real place,' Ieuan said. 'I asked him, but he was a bit evasive. This explains why.'

Tom shook his head. 'This must be from last week? He's right down to that wood now. Tonight, he'll be in among the trees. Where is it all leading to?'

Ieuan fingered the painting. Two dozen third formers crashed through the double doors outside and roared down the corridor like a tide. When the laughter had passed he said, 'You get on all right with him, don't you? When your parents got married I think they were a bit worried whether you would.'

Tom shrugged. 'It was odd at first. Especially sharing a room. We had a few flaming rows, even a fight once. But not for ages.' He grinned. 'Perhaps this dream's had one good result.'

'You must be tired, though.'

Tom nodded. 'A bit.'

'Well it's not right. He should see someone. Does his father know? Or your mother?'

'Neither.' He thought of his mother and Rhys Jones, imagined in a brief vivid moment their astonishment. 'After all, what's a dream, love?' his mother would say. 'It can't hurt you. Don't worry about it.'

'Beats me.' Ieuan said. 'But you really ought to get him to see someone. A doctor, maybe. If it goes on it could affect his health. Yours too.'

*   *   *

Too right, Tom thought on the way home, watching Simon's wan reflection in the bus window. As they got off by the pub and began the long trudge up the hill he said, 'Maybe it won't come tonight.'

'Maybe.'

They walked in silence between the grey stone walls. Once Simon stumbled, the long fringe of hair swinging into his eyes. Angrily he kicked a stone out of the way. 'Sometimes I'm almost scared to go to sleep.'

'That's daft.'

'You don't know. It doesn't happen to you.' He stopped and looked down across the valley, at the small terraces of houses and the green tumble of trees that marked the river. 'It's getting worse Tom, the further I go. But I daren't step off the road.'

'It's just a dream,' Tom growled, hating himself.

And rain began to fall on them, a stinging downpour.

*   *   *

The bedroom was dark and still; Tom drifted up to it through veils of fatigue, hauling himself stupidly to the surface. Then he lay there, half asleep. There had been some sound, something; he dragged it back to

46

his memory—a cry, a gasp. He opened his eyes and struggled up onto one elbow.

Simon was a dark huddled shape in the corner of his bed, completely still. Tom closed his eyes and listened to the slow, regular breathing. Then sleep closed over him, like a dark sea.

* * *

'Not on the table,' his mother said, whisking the *Western Mail* away and putting down the box of cereal. She went outside and they heard her calling, 'Simon! It's almost eight!'

Rhys Jones turned the paper over. 'Glamorgan are playing Saturday. We'll go, if you like?'

Tom shrugged. He knew Simon hated cricket. 'I don't mind.'

'I see they've recalled Lloyd. Now there's a mistake.'

But Tom, sprinkling sugar, was listening to his mother upstairs.

'Rhys,' she called. 'Come up here, quickly.'

Her voice sounded strange.

His stepfather went out. Tom took the paper back and began to read, but the voices upstairs, urgent and insistent, burrowed into his mind. He went out into the hall; his mother was at the telephone dialling.

'What's wrong?'

She flung him a quick, distant look. 'It's Simon. There's something the matter . . . Hello . . . yes, ambulance, please . . .'

Shock seemed to drain him of all thought. He raced upstairs and into the bedroom; Simon's father turned a white face. 'He won't wake up! We can't wake him!'

Simon lay on his side, head on one arm. He breathed evenly, his face pale, but quiet. Tom shook him and called him but nothing happened. His mother ran in behind him. 'They're coming,' she said. She went round and brushed Simon's hair from his forehead. 'Simon love,' she whispered. 'Wake up.'

When the ambulance men came Tom was ushered out. Downstairs he stacked dishes in the sink, his mind numb. There were voices, doors banging, the doctor running upstairs, his stepfather's deep, bewildered questions. He forced himself to go out in the hall; his mother ran down and grabbed his arm. 'We're going to the hospital . . . will you stay here?'

He nodded, miserably.

'You should go to school.'

'How can I?'

'All right. I'll phone. Don't worry.' She tugged her coat on and kissed him briefly. 'Don't worry. It may be nothing. I'll phone.'

When they were gone the house was silent. He sat

on the bottom of the stairs for a long time, listening to the silence. Finally he got up, washed up and made the beds. It would be all right. Simon was just tired. He would wake up and find himself in the hospital. Tom imagined the scene even to the words. Simon would ask for something to drink. He'd be surprised. Rhys would call him 'son' and joke with the nurses. Everyone would be tearful with relief.

Minute by minute, the morning dragged on, the sun altering the shadows on the mountain. He wandered from room to room, picking things up, putting them down, reading the paper, scuffing up weeds in the garden.

At ten past twelve the phone rang. His mother said, 'There's no change! He hasn't moved.'

'What do they think it is?'

'They're not sure ... doing tests, you know. All sorts of things.'

'How's Rhys?'

She sighed. 'Beside himself, quietly.'

'Can I come down?'

There was a muffled announcement from some tannoy in the background. Then she said, 'Come this afternoon. Get something to eat.'

He made some sandwiches and threw most of them away, then ran down the lane to the bus stop. It was almost an hour to Newport; the bus dawdled down the valley, between the steep green slopes of forestry. In the end he wanted to get out and run and run.

The hospital was a white maze of corridors and signs and rooms. They let him see Simon briefly; he looked so normal, just asleep, as if he would wake any minute. As Tom stood there he heard his mother rattling on nervously to the nurse in the corridor.

'... only step-brothers ... we thought when we married ... but after all they get on extremely well, better than we do ...' Then her strange gasping laugh.

At half past six they made him go home. 'I'll have to stay,' his mother said. 'Will you be all right? Shall I phone Ieuan?'

He shook his head. 'I'll manage.'

Climbing the lane to the house he paused, and leaned on a gate, watching the dusk descend slowly on the houses and the mountain. Simon was lost somewhere, lost in that other country. The doctors had murmured about comas and cataleptic states, but he knew what had happened. Simon had stepped off the road. And only he knew anything about it.

At eight o'clock he went around and locked the house up, then went upstairs to the bedroom. Deliberately, he took a pair of Simon's clean pyjamas from a drawer and put them on. Then he turned back the corner of the blue quilt and climbed into Simon's bed. It was a brass one, brought from Simon's old house. It felt hard, and a little tall.

He switched the light out and lay back. Now for the hardest part. Now he had to go to sleep.

The room was quiet; he could hear the bleat of sheep from the fields at Ty'r Nant. The bird-mobiles drifted their dim wings under the ceiling, turning and banking, wing-tip to wing-tip with their shadows.

Darkness fell on him. And sometime later, he fell asleep.

*   *   *

He was standing on the silver road. It shone, like Simon had said, but he was astonished at its brightness in the full moonlight. It was like standing on the metal bar of a brooch. The land on each side was dark, but he could smell grass and soil and some familiar, salty tang. He looked around.

'Simon?'

The wood was just ahead of him; he could touch the nearest tree-trunk. Cautiously, he walked forward.

The road glinted between wet leaves and the boles of trees. It ran downhill through the wood, often twisting back on itself, narrowing to a thread sometimes between rocks where great ferns sprouted; sometimes it was so steep that he had to hold on to branches and lower himself carefully.

At the bottom of one steep part he stopped for breath. The night was quiet around him, a murmur of leaves and rustles, the far squeak of bats.

'Simon!' he called. 'It's Tom!'

'Tom! Down here!'

The voice came from in front of him, where the path twisted sharply; beside it a sheer drop fell into darkness. Simon was a little way down, clinging to a log that seemed to have slithered down with him. If he moved, the lot might crash down.

Tom scrambled, grimly, to the very edge of the road and stopped. He dared not leave it. If he did neither of them might ever wake up.

'Are you all right?' he said, kneeling.

'Cuts, that's all. But there's nothing to hold on to.'

Tom stretched out, gripping a beech trunk with his other hand, but his fingers slid on the smooth bole. 'Wait. That's no good.'

Simon watched him. 'Don't leave the path . . .'

'I won't.'

He lay down, coiling one foot under a root. Then he slithered forward carefully, until he was hanging well over the edge, head downwards. His straining fingers touched Simon's sleeve; he grabbed tight, slid down to the wrist, then the hand. Simon edged nearer; a shower of leaves and soil slid and crashed far below.

'Now!' Tom gasped, both hands gripping tight. 'Let go!'

Simon dug his toes in and made a leap upwards; the sudden weight almost dragged Tom off the path but he hung on, gritting his teeth against the pain in his foot. There was a moment of scrambling and squirming, then slowly, between breaths, he pulled his stepbrother up the shifting bank, until they both crouched, aching, on the shining road.

'You got here,' Simon grinned, at last.

'And now I'm here,' Tom muttered, scrambling up. 'I want to see where this road leads. Don't you?'

Simon's smile faded, but he stood up.

Around the next turn of the road they found the end of the trees, and they saw with a sudden shock of delight that the sea was before them, black and shifting, the moon's track glinting across it. They could see the silver road spilling itself down the hillside, across the shingle, and right into the water that spread and ebbed over it.

'Into the sea?' Tom muttered.

'Yes, but look out there.'

Far out, dim against the dark sky, was an island. Small lights glinted on it.

'Let's go down.'

Quickly they ran to the sea's edge, into the noise of the waves crashing and sucking and rolling the pebbles of the beach. Spreading fans of water ran over their bare feet.

Tom jerked back. 'It's cold.'

Bobbing in the water, with no rope to hold it there, was a small boat, half invisible in the darkness. Two oars lay in the bottom; it seemed to have been left there for them, they thought.

Far out in the night, the lights on the island gleamed blue and green.

'Will you go?' Tom said, after a long moment.

Simon laughed briefly, and then shook his head. 'I'd like to. I mean, what's out there? How far can anyone go, into his imagination? But I know this Tom, if we did we'd never get back. Only the road is safe.'

Tom nodded. 'Do you think you'll be coming here again?'

'I doubt it.' As he spoke Simon seemed to get fainter. He laughed again. 'See you later Tom. I think someone's waking me up . . .'

When he was alone on the road Tom took one last look at the island. 'Maybe one day,' he said, quietly. Then he turned in surprise hearing the sound that had begun in the air, a high, familiar, insistent call, repeating over and over.

*   *   *

When he opened his eyes he was in bed and the telephone was ringing. For a second he lay there, watching the painted birds drift against the ceiling. Then he sat up lazily and grinned. He knew already what his mother would have to say.

Sgilti Lightfoot

'Knife has gone into meat, drink into horn, and a thronging in Arthur's court.'

'Yes, I'm sure it has,' I snapped, 'but they sent for me.'

The gatekeeper stopped picking his teeth with the point of his knife and stared. 'You? What would they want with an underfed little runt like you?'

I pushed past him. 'At least I'm not too drunk to find out.'

He aimed a kick, but I was already in the pavilion.

You could certainly have called it a thronging. Bards and harpers sang in the dim smoke; there was a magician spinning blue and green rings of light, a dog-fight, the hot stink of meat and spices, the clamour of noise and laughter and boasting—even a wrestling match, in one uproarious corner.

They were all there, all the war-band; Cai and Bedwyr, Osla Big-knife slightly drunk and waving his cup; Cynddylig the guide and Menw the spell-master; Gwalchmai with his scarlet cloak; Morgan, tall and slender, the pet snake writhing up her arm.

Arthur sat among them, his hands rubbing the carven heads on his chair, his gaze fixed and remote. Someone was talking to him, but I don't think he was listening. In all that din I doubt he could have heard. Then he saw me, and his eyes became alert, quite suddenly.

I pushed my way up to him. 'Lord?'

He gave me his hard, sombre stare. 'You're the lad Sgilti?' He twisted his head and yelled. 'Is this the boy?'

Talk subsided. The magician dropped his rings; they fell into the straw and spluttered out with a scorching hiss. Everyone looked at me.

'Yes.' Cai came and leaned on the back of the chair. 'That's him.'

For a moment I thought I had done something wrong. Then Arthur nodded.

'He's small, lithe, looks strong enough. He might do.'

Cai turned, lazily. 'Give him a drink.'

Nervously, I sipped the warm spiced wine. Outside, the sounds of the camp drifted through the noise; horses at their ropes, the eternal crackle of fires. I noticed a thin man with gangly arms sitting on a stool at Arthur's feet. He was the only one not looking at me.

'Now,' Arthur said grimly. 'How long have we been beseiging this Fortress?'

I shrugged. 'Days and nights are the same now, Lord. About a year?'

'Nearly two.' He curled his fist. 'Two years of darkness. And the Fortress not even scratched.'

I nodded, remembering the day the darkness had come, spreading and spilling over the hills and forests, like ink soaking a map. I had been outside in

58

the forge at home, and had glanced up to see what covered the sun. When I'd looked down I hadn't even been able to see the hammer I held.

Since then there had been no light. No sun, no moon, no stars, nothing to tell night from day. We lived among black fields, in rooms acrid with constant smoke. Crops curled in the furrow; cattle pined and died; birdsong was almost forgotten.

So Arthur had gathered his warband, and we had marched for ten days into the heart of the blackness and found this place—the Fortress, its black stones swallowing even the gleam of torches we held up to it. No one knew how high it was. The walls reared up, silent and empty; smooth fire-scarred blocks that grapples would not cling to, the moan of the wind sounding round them.

'There's talk,' I said doubtfully, 'in the camp. Of a sorceror . . .'

It was Cai who answered, with his sharp grin. 'We know plenty of those. Yes, we know who made the darkness. His name is Llwyd ap Cil Coed. He did something of the kind once before.' He gave a quick glance at Arthur. 'This is his revenge on us.'

Suddenly Arthur said, 'I hear you're a good tumbler. Show us.'

I stared, astonished. 'Here?'

'Now.'

The heat of the wine scorched my cheeks. I looked round; they were all watching.

'Come on,' Bedwyr snapped. 'Let's see.'

I stood up and pulled off my jerkin. Was this all they wanted then, some after-meat entertainment? Surely they had enough harpers and dancers in the camp?

The floor was clear. I stood lightly on my hands and ran a few steps, my hair falling in my eyes. Then I stood and flipped forward, once, twice, and then backwards as high and light as I could.

'Stand on one hand,' Morgan said, coming forward from the shadows.

I obeyed, lifting my left hand carefully from the ground, feeling the ache in my right, the growing wobble in my body. Quickly I rolled and jumped up.

'And is it true,' Gwalchmai asked quietly, 'that you climbed the seige ladder yesterday and jumped as it fell?'

I nodded, warily.

'You don't fear heights?'

'No, lord.'

He raised one eyebrow at Arthur.

'Oh yes,' the emperor said. 'Oh he'll do.' He glanced around; the war-band eyed each other and nodded, the edges of their faces red in the flame-light.

Arthur looked down. 'Do you agree?'

The thin man stirred. His long arms were wrapped around his knees, his fingers locked together. He shrugged. 'If he has the nerve. Which I doubt.'

I glared at him angrily. 'Whatever it is, I'm not afraid to try.'

Arthur laughed, and leaned back. 'Explain it to him.'

Cai nodded. 'Look Sgilti, all methods of attack on the Fortress have failed. Whatever sorcery guards it repels ladders and seige towers; its walls are battered with rams and missiles and magic and are not even cracked. They can't be burned, and however deep we dig we can't find their foundations. And, until now, we thought it was too smooth to climb.'

He pointed down. 'This man is called the Spider. Perhaps you can guess why.'

I did. I had begun to understand.

Morgan came and stood in front of me, one long braid of hair swinging over her shoulder. She took my hand; her fingers were long and white. 'We've used fire-arrows, to see high. There's one window that might do. It is high, very, very high. We think it might be wide enough—just—for a thin man. Or a boy.'

'That's why you want me?'

She smiled. 'Arthur has many heroes. They are all too big.' .

'We need two,' Arthur said, 'in case one falls. Someone must open the gate for us.'

I nodded, watching the Spider unfurl himself and stand, a thin, spindly man, his brown hair cropped short. 'I still say he won't make it,' he muttered.

Arthur looked at me. 'He must.'

Later, when we stood alone at the wall, I watched the man check the rope; the finest and strongest the company could find.

'Why didn't you want me?'

He looked up. 'I didn't want anyone. If you don't get up there I'll have to manage without you anyway.'

I held my anger tight inside me; a small hard knot.

The air was very cold, with little noise from the camp. Everyone was gone to the gates. The dim wall of the Fortress leaned out above me. I imagined its invisible battlements, embrasures and stairs, its remote pinnacles and airy bridges spanning the gaps from tower to tower.

The Spider flexed his arms. 'Now then.'

'Good luck.'

'I don't need luck. Keep it for yourself.'

He gave a quick spring and clung to the wall, hands and feet splayed; then began to climb with astonishing speed, feeling with fingers and elbows, toes and knees for invisible crannies. In the silence faint scuffles came down to me. For a second he even looked like a spider, a spindly jointed shape, clinging and jerking its way up into the dark.

I crouched in the lee of the wall, the wind flapping my black coat. Soon I'd have to follow—but at least I'd have the rope.

After a while I heard a faint tap, and something thudded near my feet; I groped for it and found it was a small peg. That was useless. Nothing would pierce the Fortress, Cai had said. The Spider must have found that out for himself; the tapping stopped, and there was silence.

'All right?' I whispered.

No answer. He was probably too high to hear.

I must have been half-asleep when the rope hit me silently on the shoulder; a thin line snaking down the wall. I gave it a swift tug, and felt the answering twitch. He had done it!

Quickly I looped the line round my waist, tied it tight and swung my legs up onto the wall. The rope held me, a hard ring of comfort. Arm over arm, I began to haul myself up.

It didn't take long for my arms to start getting tired. The ache grew worse, the muscles forming hard knots of pain. I stopped, swaying, gasping for cold air, but the weight seemed heavier like this. It was better to keep going, so I heaved myself up, each handgrip a terrible wrench and tug, the slither of the rope scorching through my gloves. At last, through a wave of fatigue, I felt my foot settle on something soft, like a cushion of moss on the wall. I put my weight on it; it yielded, and then held.

With a moan of relief I pulled myself upright against the wall. There were more of the things, well spaced for hands and feet. For a long time I clung there, splayed against the black surface, my cheek pressed to the damp stones. I could smell tiny lichens clinging in the crannies. Up here the wind ruffled my hair; small campfires flickered below.

After a while I felt better, and began to wonder what I was standing on. What had managed to break the sorcery of the Fortress? I slid my hand along and felt, carefully. It was something sticky; a whole mass of threads, thin and tough. I followed them, touching gently; they spread from stone to stone, stretching, like skeins of fine silk.

A web.

How had he made it?

I shivered, and at the same time the rope went taut and then tugged gently. I wound the slack tight around me. At least then if I fell I'd finish here. Better to dangle like a broken puppet than hit the ground. Then I took hold, and swung out.

The ache came back at once. Above I could see the wall jutting out steeply; I hauled myself underneath, hoping the rope had not frayed against the edge. I had to take my feet from the wall and spin giddily in the dark for a few seconds, before I could swarm up onto the overhang. There was a sloping roof, broad enough to stand on, carven with strange grinning heads. From here I could see the wall ascend again into blackness, and the ghostly line of the rope, as it passed an arrowslit just visible above.

I began to doubt then, if I could do it. Every muscle already ached; my hands were sore, my legs weak. The thought of that long fall into blackness wouldn't keep away. But I couldn't stay here. And Arthur was depending on me.

By the time I reached the arrowslit I was exhausted. My arms were leaden, wind whipped out my hair. Wedging my feet in the thin slit I hung there, careless of danger, my mind sick and spinning.

'Hurry up!' The voice hissed down the wall; glancing up I saw the window, just above, and his shadow leaning out. Then I looked down.

I've never been afraid of heights—I told the warband the truth. But that utter emptiness; the flickers of fire so far below—it made tiny cold terrors unfurl in my stomach.

Then a light was shining in my face!

With a jerk of alarm I leapt from the sill and crashed into the wall, cursing my stupidity. Inside the building a candle-flame was moving, coming closer, the glow bright in the black arrowslit.

The rope twisted and thrummed, trapping my fingers; I dragged them free and grabbed again, biting my lip from the pain. Then I clung tight, swaying.

The candle came to the window. I could see the hand that held it, a thin hand with long nails. It stayed, as if the figure waited, listening. I hung on, grimly, my hands scorching, a raw pain in my stomach. I couldn't move. I was finished.

Then the rope jerked, and I felt it rise, wonderfully, and lift me up. I was dragged up the wall in a silent series of jerks and sharp drops that sent fear gasping through me. The arrowslit fell away below. I came up through darkness, a swinging nausea of rope and stone, to a hand that grabbed me and hauled me over the sill to the solid floor, where I collapsed, a shivering heap.

'Didn't think you'd do it,' a voice muttered in my ear. 'You can let go of the rope now.'

But I had to force my fingers to open; the joints seemed set. My gloves were torn to ribbons; the skin of my palms red and sore.

'Drink this.'

The Spider's fingers offered a small flask out of the dark. The spirit in it was hot and sweet; it made me cough.

'Now, get up.' He hauled me to my feet. 'Walk about. Hurry.'

Slowly, the trembling in my legs steadied; I could stand, then walk. Beside me there was a sudden spurt of blue flame; he lit the torch and it crackled and spat, throwing red light leaping over our faces.

He looked up at me. 'I suppose I should say I was wrong.'

'You can say what you like,' I muttered, rubbing my wrenched arms. 'You could start with how you put those nets on the wall.'

I hadn't meant it to blurt out like that, but in the flamelight I saw his thin smile. 'My secret.'

'And there's someone here. Just below.' I told him about the hand that had held the candle. He shrugged, and stood up. 'We must leave that to Arthur. Our task is to find the gates.'

The torch showed we were in a small hall with thick pillars that lost themselves in the gloom overhead. There was a door in the wall, and I tried the handle, cautiously. It opened.

We looked out into a black, silent corridor. Cold airs drifted against our faces.

I walked in the Spider's long shadow, thinking of all the rooms and chambers about us; of the hand with the candle. But there was no sound; nothing leapt out at us. We felt our way down twisting stairs; through halls littered with the dark shapes of furniture; one chamber totally webbed with curtains of silk, all frayed and worn to holes, so that when I put my hand on one it crumpled, with a faint puff of sound.

As we went down, the air grew blacker. The light of the torch became pale and sickly, finally useless. The Spider threw it down in disgust and it went out. Blackness closed in.

Now we had to feel. Progress became a slow, weary shuffling, inch by inch, along an invisible wall that led us right, and left, and down endless steps.

Finally the Spider stopped, and I bumped into him.

'It's impossible,' he snarled. 'We could be anywhere! Walking in circles, no doubt.' His voice hung, as if in a high roof. We realised all at once that we were in a very large room, a hall, bitterly cold. In this place the darkness was more than lack of light; it was a breathing thing, alive, pressing against us. This was the heart of the Fortress.

Suddenly, I took my fingers off the wall and stepped away. At once I lost all bearing, was surrounded by nothing.

'Keep still,' the Spider snapped. 'If we lose each other . . .'

'We won't. You can make sure of that.'

I heard him laugh. 'Maybe. But where are you going? We need to find the gates—to go down. We should move along the wall to the next set of steps. It won't be out there in the middle.'

'Something's out there,' I whispered, staring into

the gloom. 'I know it is. I can feel it. Let me go and look. You can always pull me back.'

'No rope.'

'You don't need a rope.'

There it was again, his rustle of amusement. 'No wonder Cai picked you,' he said. 'All right. Come a bit closer.'

I moved, banging awkwardly against him. His hand groped for mine, felt down my arm. In the inky stillness he took off my glove and I felt a cold touch in the centre of my palm. A thin thread lay across my skin, slightly sticky as I touched it.

Without a word I turned and stepped out into the dark. The invisible line stretched behind me.

I had stepped into nowhere. Darkness was all about me, a weight against my hands and face; I had to wade through it, push against it. Each step was an effort. My feet slid over the smooth floor, feeling for pits and holes, deep wells that might be only inches away.

And then I bumped into something.

Heart thudding, I stopped. Faint echoes faded round the hall.

'What is it?' the Spider hissed, from far away.

'I don't know.'

Carefully, reluctantly, I put out my hand. I touched a smooth, cold surface. My fingers travelled across it, hesitantly. When I felt the other thing I jerked back, with a shiver of surprise.

After a long second I touched it again. It was an edge, a curved edge, not metal . . . wood. Gently, I fingered it. As my thumb moved up it dislodged something light and smooth that fell back into place with a click. With both hands, I felt for it.

It was a small globe, on some kind of stand. I lifted it off and held it between my palms; it was very light. My fingers arched around it. Whatever it was made of was bitterly cold; my skin stuck to it.

This was the heart of it; this small ball. I held it, while the darkness breathed around me. Then, deliberately, I let it go.

As it smashed light exploded; a scatter of glass. I stood in a sudden blinding dazzle of colour, my eyes watering with the pain, staring at a great hall, flagged with stone, hung with festoons of glorious scarlet cloth, full of the echoes of some great cry ringing from roof to floor. Before me stood a white marble table, scattered with black shiny pieces of broken glass. Behind, one hand still on the wall, his face smudged with dirt and utter astonishment, stood the Spider, and between us through the air drifted a frail silver line, glittering in the sunlight from the windows.

In all the rooms and corridors of the Fortress the echoes faded into silence.

For a second we looked at each other, too over-awed to speak. Then I wiped a dirty hand over my face and grinned at him. It would be very easy now to find the gates.

Also published by Pont Books:

Pont Books is an imprint of
Gomer Press, Llandysul